THIS COLORING BOOK BELONGS TO:

_____

Thank you for purchasing my "Animals in Costumes" coloring book! Inside, you'll find adorable animals dressed in unique and imaginative costumes, perfect for hours of creative fun. This book is part of my "Bold and Easy" series, designed to provide simple yet engaging designs that are enjoyable for all ages. If you love this book and want to explore more of my work, please check out my other titles available on Amazon. Happy coloring!
Sunflo Colors